AN UNUSUAL UNICORN

Written and Illustrated by

Christopher C. Asa

art by maya ysabel p. asa

To my beautiful wife
and three lovely kids.

Once upon a time in a magical forest, there lived shining white unicorns with bright-colored hair and magnificent ponytails.

They loved the taste of strawberries and could jump way up high.

A magical rainbow appeared once every ten years and vanished almost as quickly as it appeared.

But anyone who crossed it before disappearing would be granted a single wish by The Great Unicorn Goddess.

One day, an UNUSUAL UNICORN was born. Her coat was brown, and her hair did not shine. Her appearance was much different from the rest, but she had a special gift. She could run faster than all the other unicorns.

But, because of her looks, the other unicorns laughed at her, making her feel sad and rejected.

So, one day, she ran as fast as she could away from the magical forest.

Along her way, she met a delightful young girl who loved horses. The girl told the unicorn of her dreams to become an amazing painter, despite her inability to see colors because she was color blind.

They quickly became good friends.

The two of them pranced along and celebrated each other's differences as they spent their days together.

But the unicorn remained sad because of her different appearance. So, one day, she decided to return home and attempt to cross the magical rainbow. She dreamed of changing her appearance and fitting in with all the other unicorns.

When she returned, the other unicorns immediately started making fun of her. But she waited for the rainbow.

And she waited.

Finally, the magical rainbow appeared!
She ran as fast as her legs would carry her
to make it to the rainbow before it
disappeared.

Because of her remarkable speed, she made it!

The Great Unicorn Goddess bestowed upon her a single wish.

The unicorn was about to make the wish she had been dreaming of, but suddenly, she remembered her wonderful friend who wanted nothing more than to paint beautiful, colorful art.

So, instead of using the wish on herself,
she wished for her friend's eyes to be cured.

She soon went to visit her friend again. She was so happy to see that her friend had become a wonderful painter, just like she had dreamed of becoming.

Her friend's charming artwork
of flowers and horses took her breath away.

To thank the unicorn for such a remarkable gift, the girl created a painting of her flowing hair and stunning body. The girl captured her dear friend's essence and painted her with spectacular, shining colors.

The unicorn's different appearance
no longer made her feel sad. Instead,
she felt magical and special.